Written by
Jane Clarke

Illustrated by
Cathy Gale

Plodney Creeper, Supersloth

Blue Bananas

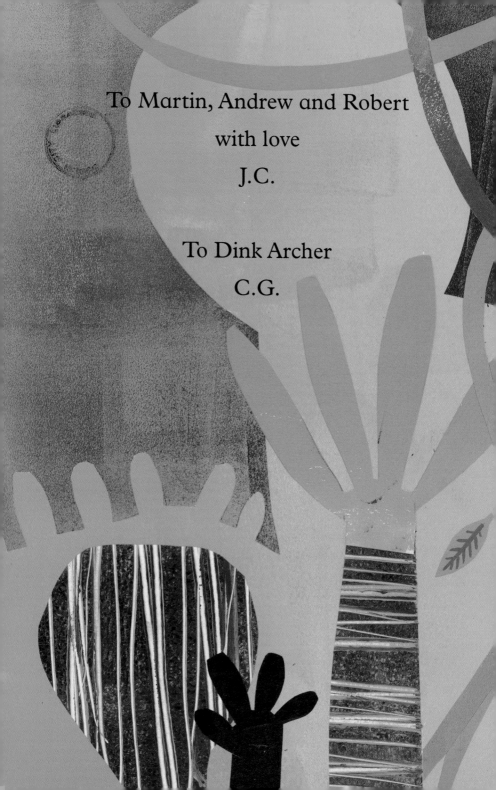

To Martin, Andrew and Robert
with love
J.C.

To Dink Archer
C.G.

'Ye-hah!'

Plodney crashed through the branches. A shower of leaves fell on to the sloths below.

'I'm worried about Plodney,'
Mrs Creeper said. 'I think he might be
a bit . . .' She caught a leaf and chewed
it slowly. There was a far-away look
in her eyes.

On the branch above her, Plodney

stopped swinging. He held his breath.

'A bit what, dear?' Mrs Clinger asked.

Mrs Creeper lowered her voice.

'A bit . . . *fast*.'

'*Fast*? Dearie me!' Mrs Clinger said.

'A sloth should never be *fast*!'

'If only Plodney was as slow as Layzee,' Mrs Creeper sighed. 'Look at her lovely green hair. Only the slowest sloths have green hair.'

'You're quite right, dear,' Mrs Clinger said. 'My Layzee is very slow. She hardly ever moves. I am so proud of her.'

Mrs Creeper yawned and shut her eyes. 'I get tired just looking at Plodney,' she said.

Th-u-nk.

Plodney crashed down between them.

The branch swayed.

'Hello!' he grinned.

Oops!

Mrs Creeper and Mrs Clinger shuddered.

Layzee opened one eye.

'Oh Plodney,' his
mother groaned,
'when will you learn to
hang around?'
'Don't worry, dear,'
Mrs Clinger said.
'He'll learn to do that at
school, won't he?'

11

It was dawn. The rainforest was waking up. It rang with the calls of birds and animals greeting the new day.

Only the sloths slept on.

Plodney swung up the creaky School Branch. 'Good morning, Mr Gripper!'

'Early for school, again!' the headmaster grumbled. 'That's every day this week. You must try harder to be late. Remember Plodney, SLOTHS ARE SLOW!'

Every morning Miss Snailspace's class did Sleeping and Hanging Around. They were all very good at it, except for Plodney.

He did his best,

but it was no good.

Plodney could not keep still.

ye-hah!

'Plodney moved again!' Slo-Mo said.

'We should call him Speedy!'

'Or Flash,' Layzee said.

The whole class laughed.

Plodney's wriggling!

He never stops!

Not like us!

At last it was playtime.

'Ye-hah!' Plodney yelled. He grabbed a creeper. 'Let's play Tarzan of the Jungle!'

Me, Tarzan!

'Only fast sloths like to play Tarzan of the Jungle,' Layzee said. 'We all want to play Dead Jaguars.'

'That's right, Speedy!' Slo-Mo said.

'But we *always* play Dead Jaguars,' complained Plodney.

'No we don't,' said Layzee.

'Sometimes we play Statues.'

'Plodney, you moved,' Slo-Mo said.

He was the first one out as usual.

18

Layzee didn't move
for over three hours.
Layzee won.
'I'm the slowest sloth
in school,' she boasted.

'It's not fair,' Plodney told Miss
Snailspace. 'I'll never be as slow as
Layzee.'

'We can't all be as
slow as Layzee,'
Miss Snailspace
said.

After school Miss Snailspace had a word
with Plodney and his mother.
'I know Plodney finds it hard to slow
down, but he is doing his best,' she said.

I must stay
still. I must
stay still.

'I am very pleased to have him in my class. I think he is a super sloth.'

Plodney felt very proud. Miss Snailspace thought he was a Supersloth! One day Plodney Creeper, 'Supersloth', would show the world what he could do.

The next day, thunder rolled around the rainforest. The sloths were at school.

They were all doing Sleeping.

All but Plodney.

He was listening to the sounds

of the rainforest.

The birds were singing.

The monkeys were hooting.

The frogs were croaking.

They were enjoying the rain.

Cr-a-a-a-ck.

Suddenly, the sky lit up with a flash of
lightning.

'Wake up! Wake up!' Plodney shouted.

'School Branch has been hit!'

The sloths slept on.

They were very good at Sleeping.

It was their favourite subject.

Cr-e-e-e-ak.

This time the sloths woke up. 'School Branch is breaking!' Plodney yelled. 'Use the creepers to swing across to the trunk!'

Quick. Get moving!

'*Swing*? We've never done *Swinging*,' Layzee said. 'We're not all fast like you, you know.'

27

I must get a grip.

I've gone weak at the knees!

'You can do it!' Plodney said. 'Mr Gripper and Miss Snailspace will swing across first and catch you.'

Miss Snailspace looked nervously at Mr Gripper. Mr Gripper was trembling. Plodney handed them a creeper.

'Ye-hah!' said Miss Snailspace weakly.

They landed in a tangled heap on the

tree trunk.

'Send them over!' Mr Gripper shouted. 'Hurry up!'

The sloths looked at each other in amazement. They had never heard Mr Gripper tell anyone to hurry up before. Two at a time, the sloths swung across to safety.

Don't worry, Layzee. I'll be back!

Mr Gripper and Miss Snailspace caught

them as they landed on the trunk.

At last it was Plodney and Layzee's turn.

All the best creepers had been used.

Plodney swung along the branch

to find a creeper strong

enough for two.

Cr-e-e-a-a-ack.

School Branch gave way.

'Hang on, Layzee!' Plodney yelled.

School Branch dropped like a stone

towards the forest floor.

T-h-w-ack!

School Branch stopped falling. It was

caught in a tangle of creepers.

Pop. Pop. Pop-pop-pop.

One by one, the creepers broke.

'Hold tight!' yelled Plodney.

The end of School Branch hit the

forest floor with a cru-u-u-n-ch.

The leaves swished.

'Layzee! Are you okay?'

There was no sign of her. She must

have lost her grip! She might be hurt.

Plodney stood up and looked around.

Where was she? He couldn't see

anything. He couldn't hear anything.

All the animals were still.

The rainforest was silent.

What was wrong?

There she was! Layzee lay on her
back in the shadows of the trees.
'Are you okay?' Plodney called.
'I . . . I think so. I didn't fall far.'
Layzee tried to get to her feet but
her arms and legs were too weak.
She had been doing too much
Hanging Around.

Deep in the shadows, something stirred.

A dark shape slunk towards Layzee. Its emerald green eyes glittered.

The jaguar crouched, ready to pounce.

Quick as a flash, Plodney ran towards

Layzee. The jaguar sprang.

Just in time, Plodney pulled Layzee out of its way. The jaguar hissed with rage.

'Hang on to me!' Plodney dragged Layzee up the tree.

The jaguar leapt on to the branch beside them. It crouched low against the wood. Plodney grabbed a creeper. 'Ye-hah!' he yelled. The jaguar leapt after them. Plodney and Layzee swung across to another branch.

The jaguar missed its footing and fell to the forest floor. It circled the tree looking puzzled and limped away.

They got away! How strange.

'Phew,' said Layzee. 'I bet that jaguar was surprised to meet such a fast sloth!' 'Supersloths are always fast,' Plodney said.

Plodney was having a great time.

They were playing a new game called

Supersloth. They had to use creepers to

swing all the way around the tree.

The winner would be the first one back.

Today Plodney Creeper, 'Supersloth',

was going to win.

'Ye-hah!' Plodney yelled as he launched himself on a creeper.

'Ye-hah!' yelled Layzee, Dawdle, Hanga and Slo-Mo as they tried to keep up with him.

Slow down, Superplod.

He's the fastest!

And the greatest!

'It makes me tired just to look at them,'

Mrs Creeper yawned.

'Me too, dear,' Mrs Clinger said.

'But we are all very grateful to

Plodney. You must be so proud of him.'

'I'm always proud of Plodney,' said Mrs
Creeper. She shut her eyes and smiled.
'He is a super sloth, you know.'